PUFFIN BOOKS

Published by the Penguin Group
Penguin Books Ltd, 80 Strand, London WC2R 0RL, England
Penguin Putnam Inc., 375 Hudson Street, New York, New York 10014, USA
Penguin Books Australia Ltd, 250 Camberwell Road, Camberwell, Victoria 3124, Australia
Penguin Books Canada Ltd, 10 Alcorn Avenue, Toronto, Ontario, Canada M4V 3B2
Penguin Books India (P) Ltd, 11 Community Centre, Panchsheel Park, New Delhi – 110 017, India
Penguin Books (NZ) Ltd, Cnr Rosedale and Airborne Roads, Albany, Auckland, New Zealand
Penguin Books (South Africa) (Pty) Ltd, 24 Sturdee Avenue, Rosebank 2196, South Africa

Penguin Books Ltd, Registered Offices: 80 Strand, London WC2R 0RL, England

www.penguin.com

First published 2002
Published in this edition 2003
1 3 5 7 9 10 8 6 4 2

Copyright © Chris Riddell, 2002
All rights reserved

The moral right of the author/illustrator has been asserted

Manufactured in China

British Library Cataloguing in Publication Data
A CIP catalogue record for this book is available from the British Library

ISBN 0–140–56778–X

Platypus

CHRIS RIDDELL

and the Lucky Day

PUFFIN BOOKS

Platypus found a banana he had forgotten about under his pillow. "Today must be my lucky day," he said, jumping out of bed.

"Today is a perfect day for kite flying," said Platypus.

But the string on
his kite was tangled up.

"Lucky I have some spare
string in my collecting
box," he said.

Platypus went
outside to
fly his kite.

It was very windy
but he held on
tight until . . .

... SNAP! The string broke.

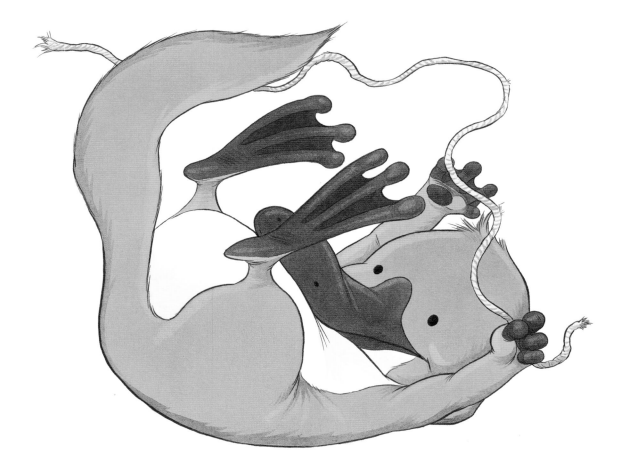

"Lucky that tree was there to catch my kite,"
said Platypus looking up into the branches.

He started to climb the tree. His fingertips could just touch the kite but . . .

... CRACK! The branch broke.

"What a perfect day for painting pictures," said Platypus.

He got out his paints and his painting apron.

Platypus painted a beautiful picture, but just as he was colouring in the sky . . .

. . . there was a sudden gust of wind.

"Oh no!" said Platypus.
"Lucky I was wearing
my apron."

But his lovely
painting was ruined.

Then it began to rain,

very hard.

Platypus ran indoors.

He tripped up on the old kite string
and bumped his head.

"I was wrong," sniffed Platypus sadly. "Today is not my lucky day."

"I'm going back to bed!" he said.

Platypus found the banana he'd forgotten about under his pillow. He ate it and began to feel a little better.

He found Bruce too, under the duvet.

"I thought I'd lost you!" he said, hugging Bruce.
He began to feel a lot better.

Outside, it was still raining. "What a perfect day for tidying my cupboard," said Platypus.

He found all sorts of things
he'd forgotten about,

or tidied away,

or thought were
broken . . .

. . . but found he could mend.

Best of all, Platypus found his special hat.

The rain stopped and the sun came out. "What a perfect day for go-carting!" said Platypus running outside. He climbed to the top of the hill.

"Whee!" he laughed, whizzing down the hill. His hat slipped over his eyes and he couldn't see where he was going.

BUMP! Platypus crashed into a tree.

Something landed in his lap. "My kite!"
said Platypus excitedly. "This is
my lucky day after all."